S0-ANO-619

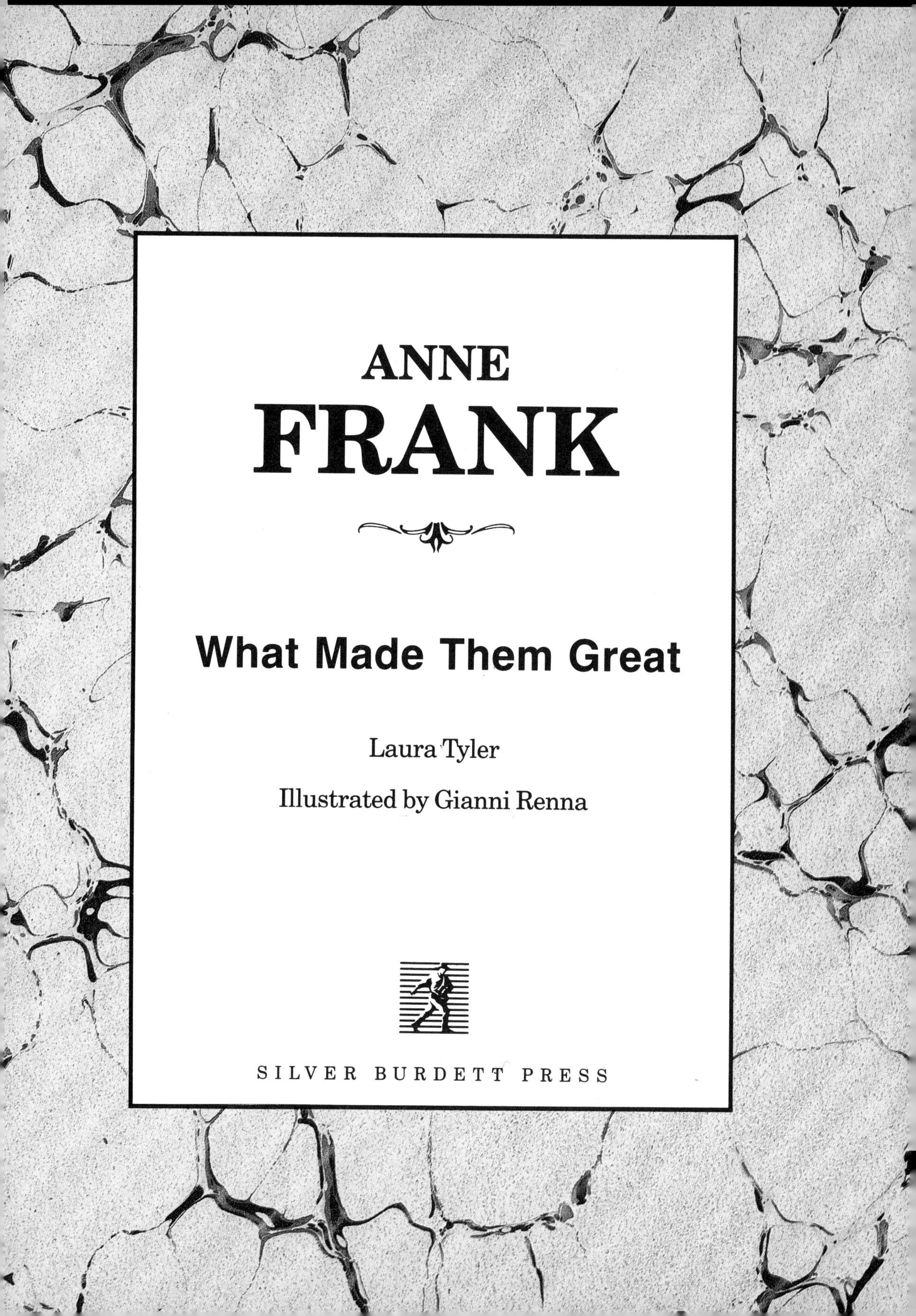

ANNE FRANK

What Made Them Great

Laura Tyler

Illustrated by Gianni Renna

SILVER BURDETT PRESS

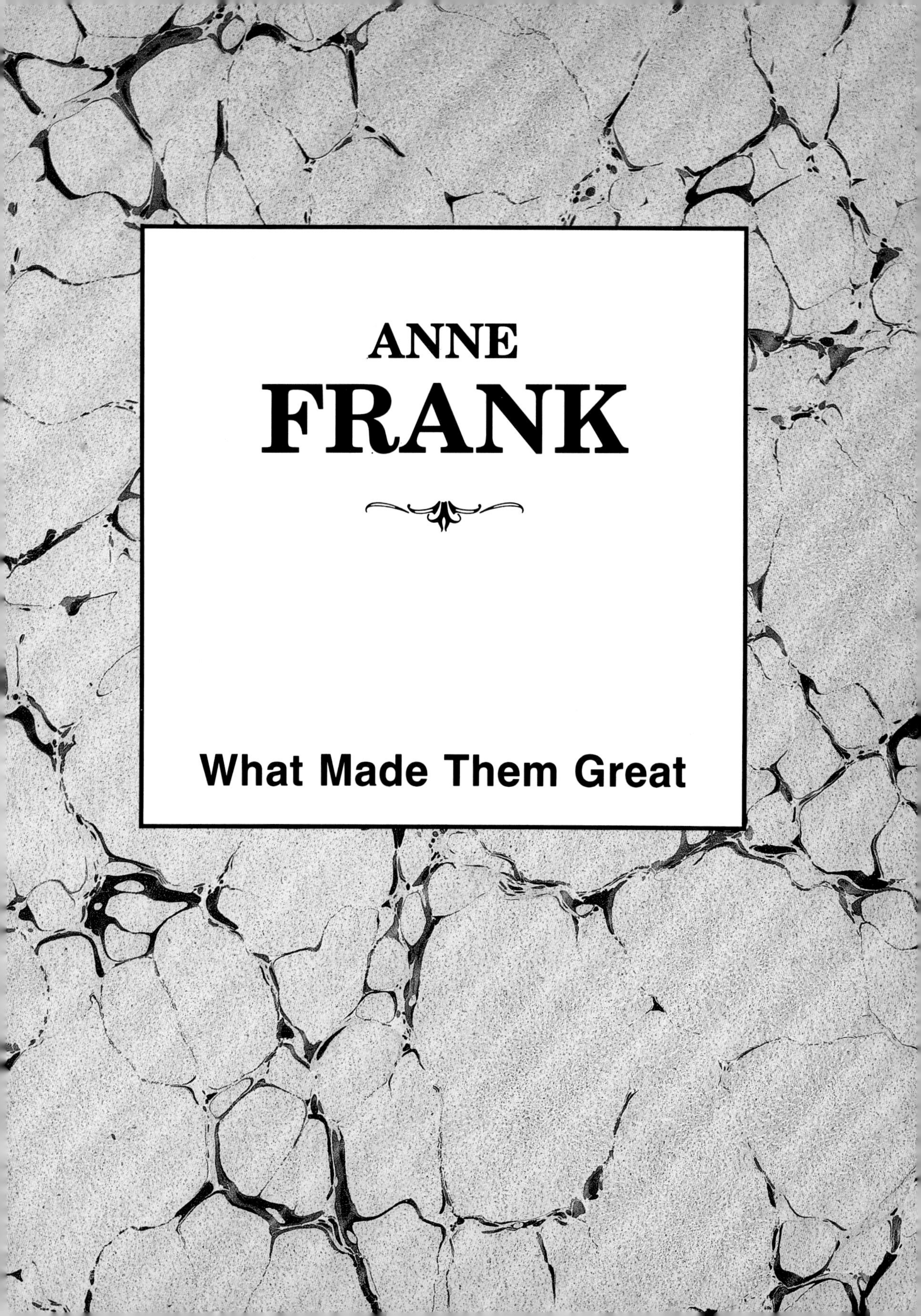

ANNE FRANK

What Made Them Great

ACKNOWLEDGMENTS

We would like to thank Daniel Horn, Department of History, Rutgers University and Craighton Hippenhammer, Cuyahoga County Public Library, Ohio for their guidance and helpful suggestions.

Project Editor: Emily Easton (Silver Burdett Press)

Adapted and reformatted from the original by Kirchoff/Wohlberg, Inc.

Project Director: John R. Whitman
Graphics Coordinator: Jessica A. Kirchoff
Production Coordinator: Marianne Hile

Library of Congress Cataloging-in-Publication Data

Tyler, Laura,
Anne Frank/Laura Tyler; illustrated by Gianni Renna.
p. cm.—[FROM SERIES: What Made Them Great]

Adaptation of: Anna Frank/Lina Tridenti; translated by Stephen Thorne.
© 1985 Silver Burdett Company, Morristown, New Jersey.
[FROM SERIES: Why They Became Famous]
Includes bibliographical references.
Summary: Traces the life of the Jewish girl who hid with seven other people in an attic for two years in Nazi-occupied Holland and chronicled her day-to-day life in a diary which was discovered after her death in a German concentration camp.
1. Frank, Anne, 1929-1945—Juvenile literature. 2. Holocaust, Jewish (1939-1945)—Netherlands—Amsterdam—Biography—Juvenile Literature. 3. Jews—Netherlands—Amsterdam—Biography—Juvenile literature. 3. Jews—Netherlands—Amsterdam—Biography—Juvenile literature. 4. Amsterdam (Netherlands)—Biography—Juvenile literature. [1. Frank, Anne, 1929-1945. 2. Jews—Biography. 3. Holocaust, Jewish (1939-1945)—Netherlands—Amsterdam—Biography.] I. Renna, Gianni, ill. II. Tridenti, Lina, Perché Sono Diventati Famosi, Anna Frank. III. Title. IV. Series.

DS135.N6T95 1990 940.53′18′092—dc20 [B] [92] 89-77115 CIP AC

 Published by Silver Burdett Press, a division of Simon & Schuster, Inc. Englewood Cliffs, New Jersey. Manufactured in Italy.

Translated into English by Stephen Thorne for Silver Burdett Press
from Perché Sono Diventati Famosi: Magellano
First published in Italy in 1982 by Fabbri Editori S.p.A., Milan

10 9 8 7 6 5 4 3 2 1 (Library Binding)
10 9 8 7 6 5 4 3 2 (Softcover)

ISBN 0-382-09975-3 (Library Binding)
ISBN 0-382-24002-2 (Softcover)

TABLE OF CONTENTS

Leaving Germany

ach evening, Anne would wait in the garden for her father to come home from work. On her fifth birthday, she was bursting with excitement. That evening, she ran to meet her father. She could hardly wait to show him a lovely doll she had just received.

Under her father's arm was a package wrapped in brightly colored paper. Anne spotted it at once. She loved birthdays, and she adored special treats. "Is that for me?" she cried happily.

On his way home, her father had stopped at a bookshop. When Anne tore off the wrappings, she beamed with pleasure. Then and there, she made her father read her a story.

Anne Frank was born on June 12, 1929, in Frankfurt, Germany. Her father, Otto Frank, was a businessman. She had one sister, Margot, who was three years older than she was. Both her mother and father came from families that had been well off at one time.

The Franks were Jews. They were devout members of the Jewish religion. Numerous Jewish people made their home in Germany at that time. Many had lived there for generations. But, by 1930, terrible things were going on. Life became not only unpleasant, but dangerous.

Something took place in Germany to change the situation for the Franks—and for all Jews. The Nazi Party had begun to gain political popularity. Soon, Jews faced all sorts of unfair treatment. At first, their civil and political rights were taken away. As time went on, the persecution got worse. Finally, they would even be denied the right to earn a decent living.

In 1933, Adolf Hitler became head of the government. Hitler believed that native, Aryan (white), gentile (non-Jewish) Germans were better than all other peoples. The Jews, especially, were wrongly considered inferior. Once Hitler seized power, laws were passed that forbade Jews to hold public office. Jews who worked in professions such as teaching found themselves out of jobs.

All over Germany, the streets became unsafe for Jews. Men in brown uniforms beat them up. Sometimes, the Nazis even killed people, and nobody stopped them. They smashed store windows. They burned synagogues—the Jewish places of worship. Life in Germany became a living nightmare.

As time went on, the Nazi nightmare extended beyond the Jewish community. Thousands of other people who appeared "different"—in any way—became targets of Nazi persecution. Horrible prisons, called "concentration camps," were built.

First, Jews were arrested and shipped off to these frightening camps. Soon, others followed.

Thousands of gypsies were arrested, because they were seen as "different." Over time, thousands of homosexuals were arrested also, because they, too, were seen as "different." Eventually, anyone who did not support Hitler and his policies could expect to be arrested without just cause.

Throughout these nightmare years, Jews continued to be persecuted the most. Before the nightmare ended, millions of innocent people—men, women, and children—were tortured and killed in the Nazi's camps. Eventually, this inhumane program of extermination would come to be known as the "Holocaust." It is certainly the darkest period of modern history.

In 1935, the "Nuremburg Laws" were passed. These new laws took away from all Jews their rights of German citizenship. By the time this happened, however, the Frank family had already escaped from Nazi Germany.

When Anne was four years old, her parents decided to move to a safer country. Even though they were not rich, they luckily had enough money to go to Holland. Their new home was the city of Amsterdam. Here, Mr. Frank went into business importing spices and jellies. He became a partner in the firm of Kohlen and Company. Soon, the Franks were doing well again.

Everyone spoiled Anne because she was the youngest. Leaving Germany had affected her much

less than her sister. Margot always tended to be quiet and serious. Anne was the bubbly one. Both Anne and Margot attended a Montessori school.

When Anne was ten, her grandmother came to live with them. Her grandmother's arrival was especially enjoyable for Anne. Granny told the most wonderful stories.

One day, though, Anne found her grandmother in tears. "Are you thinking about Auntie and Uncle again?" Anne asked. "They're safe in America."

"I'll never see them again," her grandmother sobbed. "The war has begun. Who knows how it will end?"

Anne felt confused. She had heard nothing about a war. "But where is the war?" she asked. "And who started it?"

Fighting had not actually begun yet, her grandmother explained. But Hitler had decided to grab any country in which Germans were living. Already, he had taken over Austria and sent his armies into Czechoslovakia.

"But why?" Anne asked.

"He wants to build a powerful empire," she replied. "Now the whole world is afraid of him."

Anne felt alarmed. Hitler had gobbled up Austria and Czechoslovakia simply because Germans lived there. What other countries might he decide to attack next?

The Germans Arrive

n September 1, 1939, the German Army moved into Poland. The invasion came from both land and air. Although the Poles fought bravely, they were no match for Hitler's war machine. After a month, Poland surrendered.

That was just the beginning. Seven months later, German soldiers marched into Scandinavia. Finland fell in March 1940. In no time, Denmark and Norway had been conquered. Next, the Germans turned their gaze to the west. They were determined to take France. But the countries of Luxembourg, Holland, and Belgium stood in their way.

On May 14, 1940, Holland surrendered. This allowed Hitler's army to press forward into France. Nowhere did the Germans meet with much resistance. It seemed as if Hitler could not be stopped. By the end of June, German tanks were rolling down the broad boulevards of Paris.

The worst fears of Anne's grandmother had come to pass. Seven years after fleeing Germany, the Franks found themselves once again living under German rule. Yet again, they were being persecuted because they were Jews. Each day, their lives grew more restricted. Their freedoms were snatched away. Overnight, Amsterdam had turned into a city of fear.

Everyone who was a Jew had to sew a yellow cloth star on his or her clothing. This was to distinguish them from people who were not Jewish.

Mr. Frank tried to hide his fears around the girls and their grandmother. He saw no reason to alarm them. But with his friends, it was different.

In his business, Otto Frank had several close friends—Mr. Van Daan, Mr. Kraler, and Mr. Koophuis. Whenever these gentlemen came to visit, the main topic of conversation was events taking place in Germany. Especially alarming were the persecutions against Jews. The Nazis continued to loot shops of Jewish merchants and set fire to Jewish homes. There were even more terrible rumors of prison camps. But perhaps the camps were only exaggerations. At this early stage, it was hard to know for certain.

One evening, Mr. Kraler was outraged. He shouted, "Have you heard the latest? Now they're going after synagogues and cemeteries!"

Mrs. Frank shook her head. "Now it will happen here, too," she said.

"No," her husband hurried to say. "It's different here. The Germans are just passing through."

But Mr. Van Daan disagreed. "We mustn't fool ourselves," he warned. "Jews have been sent to concentration camps ever since Hitler took over."

Mr. Koophuis insisted that this couldn't be so. If any Jews were arrested, they surely could not have been ordinary people. They must have been political troublemakers or common criminals.

The argument grew heated. "Absolutely not," shouted Mr. Van Daan. "They hate the Jews simply because they *are* Jews!"

After Mrs. Frank had gone to bed, the men went on talking. "Wasn't it best to face the facts?" Mr. Frank asked. "What had happened to Jews living in other countries conquered by the Nazis?" The answer was clear—they were suffering horribly.

Mr. Frank told his friends that they should use their energy to do something useful. If trouble should arrive, they must be prepared. What they needed was a safe hiding place.

"But where?" Mr. Van Daan's neck slumped. "There's no way out," he said in despair. "We'll all end up in the concentration camps."

Europe was at war. Great Britain and France had been drawn into the conflict. But so far, they had not been able to organize their forces. Hitler remained victorious.

The Franks received sad news. Some of their friends back in Germany had been chased out of the country and forbidden, ever, to return. The report greatly distressed Anne's grandmother. Each day, she looked older and more frail.

Daily life in Amsterdam seemed to go on much as usual. Everything appeared to be normal. But the German occupation was like an invisible black cloud hanging over the city.

Spring came to Amsterdam. One Sunday morning, Anne and her father went out for a stroll. The sun was lovely. Red and yellow tulips lined the sidewalks. The squares were crowded with people.

"How are things at school?" Mr. Frank asked his daughter. Anne was a bright student, but sometimes she got into trouble with her teacher. She had a bad habit of talking in class. As punishment, her

teacher made her write compositions. Once, she had to write on the subject of "A Chatterbox." Another time, it was "The Incurable Chatterbox."

And now, she told her father, there was still another essay due. The silly title of this one was "Quack, Quack, Quack Said Little Miss Goose."

They walked along laughing. The day was perfect. The whole city was a mass of blossoms. Anne had come to love Amsterdam. She could not help exclaiming, “What a wonderful city!”

“Wonderful,” Mr. Frank agreed. “What a pity it’s no longer free.”

A Loss of Freedom

nne and Mr. Frank continued their walk around the city. It was not hard for Anne to imagine what her father was thinking. They came to a park. A large sign had been posted where everyone would notice. It warned that Jews were forbidden to enter. The park was reserved for people who were not Jews.

The sign made Anne stop and stare. "So many things are forbidden," she cried out softly.

Jews had to wear the yellow "Star of David." But that was only the beginning, it turned out. Almost every day, some new restriction was issued. It was very annoying. For example, Jews were forbidden to play sports or to attend movies and theaters. All shopping had to be done in Jewish stores, between the hours of three and five in the afternoon.

Even getting from one place to another was hard now. They were not allowed to use the city streetcars or their own bicycles. Driving a car was no longer permitted either. And now, it would be impossible to meet friends and walk in the park.

"But why?" Anne asked her father.

"So that the Germans can always keep an eye on us."

That made Anne angry. "What are we allowed to do?" she asked.

"Be together," her father answered. "At least we're allowed to return to our home."

Anne fell silent. Then she said, "Daddy, why do the Germans hate us so much?"

Mr. Frank explained how the Romans had sent the Jews away from Palestine in 66 B.C. The Jews had found new homes all over the world. But wherever they went, the Jews remained true to their faith and their traditions. Always, the Jews faced serious problems. They had to struggle to live. Frequently, they became very good businesspeople and traders. But then, they would be hated for their success. Over the centuries, they were often mistreated.

"Why did so many Jews choose business?" Anne wondered.

"Because life has always been uncertain for us," Mr. Frank replied. "Jews discovered it was better not to own property. They invested in goods that could be easily moved." He added that Jews became money lenders (bankers), because Christians were forbidden to do it.

At the start of the occupation, the Germans pretended to be agreeable. They tried to win the

goodwill of the Dutch people. Obviously, it would mean less trouble for them if everyone cooperated. However, this turned out to be unrealistic. The Dutch fought back whenever they could.

At the first sign of disobedience, the Germans changed their tactics. They got tough. First, they threatened. Then, they began to dole out harsh punishments. They threw people into prison. Any actions whatsoever against the Nazis meant that prisoners would be killed.

Anne was in sixth grade by now. Ever since coming to Amsterdam, she and her sister had always attended the same Montessori school. But even that was about to change.

One morning, the head of the school came into Anne's classroom. She was to teach 6B its last lesson before school ended for the year. But Anne knew it would be the last lesson she would ever have there. When the class was over, the headmistress made an announcement. "I have some sad news," she said. "Anne must go to another school next year. But all of us wish her well."

The children turned to Anne in surprise. Where was she going?

"To the Jewish Secondary School," Anne said.

But nobody could understand the reason.

The headmistress told them, "Because the occupation laws say that she must." She reached out her hand to Anne and embraced her affectionately.

Anne had been only a little girl when she came to the school. She had grown up there.

The teacher turned to the class. "History is teaching us a hard lesson," she said.

Anne's classmates felt stunned. And Anne herself could not control her emotions. She bowed her head and wept.

Finally, the headmistress took Anne by the hand. "Come along," she said. "Margot is waiting for you." At the door, she hugged her student.

Margot was standing at the entrance of the school. She, too, had tears in her eyes. Hand in hand, they walked home.

It was the beginning of school vacation. But this year, Anne could take little pleasure in the holiday from studies.

In the autumn, Anne and Margot entered the Jewish Secondary School. Anne missed her old friends at Montessori. But before long, she adjusted to the new school. She made new friends. The teachers turned out to be excellent, too. Despite a few problems with algebra, Anne managed to get high marks.

Another year went by. Anne's grandmother died. Afterwards, Anne felt sad and lonely. Otherwise, nothing very unusual happened. The laws against the Jews did not get any better. But for a while, they did not become any worse either. Everything considered, Anne felt quite happy.

A Special Birthday Present

June 12, 1942, was Anne's thirteenth birthday. That morning she woke early. Her cat, Moortje, greeted her with his usual "meows." She stooped down and picked him up. Then, she went down the hall and knocked on the door of her parents' room.

Soon, everyone was trooping into the parlor. Margot, barely awake, appeared in her nightdress. Waiting for Anne were flowers and cakes, as well as a stack of gifts. Anne opened the parcels carefully, so as not to rip the pretty paper and ribbons.

One of the gifts turned out to be very special. The package looked like a book. But instead, Anne discovered that it was a diary. She thought it was perfectly marvelous.

"My first diary!" she exclaimed happily. "I'm going to write all my secrets in it. And woe to anyone who tries to read it!"

That very day, she began recording her daily thoughts and activities in her own diary.

From the start, Anne regarded the diary as quite special. She wasn't *just* going to write down what she did every day. That would be too boring. Instead, she decided to think of it as her closest,

dearest friend. Although she had made friends at her new school, there was no one to whom she could tell absolutely *everything*.

"From now on," she promised herself, "my diary will be just like a best girlfriend." She even gave her new "friend" a name—"Kitty."

In 1942, life became truly unbearable for the Jews of Amsterdam. There were harsh new laws. Jews were now forbidden to work in business. Mr. Frank was forced to leave his job at Kohlen and Company. Mr. Koophuis and Mr. Kraler, who were Christians, had to carry on without him. With no work to keep him busy, he stayed at home all day. Luckily, it was school vacation for his daughters. They were able to spend time together.

One morning, Mr. Frank took Anne for a walk. He decided to tell her about a secret plan. "The day may soon come when we will have to hide," he said quietly. "If that time *should* ever arrive, the family must be prepared."

There were two terrible things that could happen. The Germans might seize their money and property. But even worse, the Germans could arrest them. For many months, Mr. Frank had been transferring their valuable belongings to his Dutch friends. If the Germans made trouble for the Franks, they would simply disappear. Mr. Frank had arranged a hideaway where he believed the Nazi secret police could not find them.

The thought of running away filled Anne with awful dread.

What terrified the Jews the most was to be summoned to Nazi headquarters. A notice would be sent out ordering a person to register for work. By now, everyone knew these notices were a trick. They really meant being arrested and taken away to a concentration camp.

On Sunday, July 5, Margot Frank received a notice. The next day, she was to report to Nazi headquarters. When Anne heard this, she burst into tears. Her sister was only sixteen. How dare the Nazis take a young girl from her family?

"She isn't going," Mrs. Frank declared. She told the girls to collect their most precious belongings. Just a very few things could be taken, only what would fit into a small bag. They were going into hiding, immediately.

Anne ran from room to room, stuffing things into her schoolbag. One of the things she packed was her diary. Later that day, Mr. Frank's secretary came by. Recently married, Miep was with her new husband, Henk Van Santen. Miep and Henk filled their bags and pockets with clothing and provisions. They made two trips to the hiding place.

On Monday morning, Mrs. Frank woke the girls at five-thirty. "Hurry," she urged.

They were to pile on as much clothing as possible. A Jew carrying suitcases would have

aroused suspicion. Quickly, Anne pulled on several undershirts, a dress, a jacket, two pairs of stockings. One layer went on top of another. That morning, the weather was cool and wet. Perhaps it would not look strange to be seen wearing coats.

Margot was the first to leave. She took a bulky satchel of books. Miep went with her.

Anne waited silently. She stooped to pet Moortje, the cat. The thought of leaving Moortje behind was awful. But neighbors had promised to look after him. She knew he would be well cared for.

At seven o'clock it was time to go. She went around the house, saying good-bye to the familiar rooms. Then, she kissed Moortje and walked out the door with her parents.

It was raining. The streets were just beginning to fill with people going to work. As the Franks walked along, their yellow stars drew a few stares. Some people nodded in greeting, as if to express sympathy for their troubles. But Anne and her parents trudged on in silence, pretending not to notice. They were careful to avoid the main streets.

At last, Anne realized where they were going. Even though their route had wound through the back streets, they were now on Prinsengracht Canal. To her surprise, they were approaching the building where her father had worked.

"Father," she whispered, "do you mean we're going to live in your office?"

Life in Hiding

he offices of Kohlen and Company were located in an old four-story building. On the ground floor was a warehouse. Upstairs on the first floor were offices. On the second and third floors, at the back of the building, were the secret rooms.

To reach the hiding place, it was necessary to pass through corridors and storerooms. Anne and her parents climbed the wooden staircase to the second floor. On the small landing were two doors. The one on the left led to the attics at the front of

the building. The other door
led to the hideaway. Later, the entrance
to the hideaway would be covered by a bookcase.

For many months, Otto Frank and his friends had been preparing for this day. The apartment was carefully planned. It was divided between the second and third floors. There were three small rooms on the lower floor. Anne's parents had one of them. Next door was Anne and Margot's room. Adjoining the girls' room was a tiny, windowless room with a washbasin and toilet.

A steep flight of stairs led to the upper floor. Here was a large room that contained a sink and a gas oven. This room could be used as a parlor and kitchen. There was also a cramped hall room and an attic.

That rainy Monday morning, the apartment seemed especially sad and bare. In no way did it look like a home. Mrs. Frank kept gazing around. It was clear that she felt terribly discouraged. Without saying a word, she sank down on a chair. Everything had happened so quickly. Overnight, their lives had been turned upside down. Mrs. Frank had trouble taking it all in.

Anne found her sister and Miep hard at work. There was so much to do. First, the whole place had to be scrubbed. Then, boxes of food were unpacked and stored. Their belongings had to be put in order.

The first few days were devoted to making the hideaway into a home. There was very little space. But everyone felt lucky to be safe. Downstairs in the offices were Miep, Mr. Kraler, and Mr. Koophuis. It was comforting to know that their friends were working close by.

A week went by. On July 13, the Franks were joined by another family. Mr. Van Daan had worked with Anne's father. With him was his wife and fifteen-year-old son, Peter. Now, there were seven refugees occupying the secret apartment.

As the days passed, the Franks and the Van Daans began to organize their lives. In addition to Miep and their friends, others worked in the offices below. Of course, these people knew nothing about the hideaway. It would be very dangerous if they ever suspected the existence of the refugees. That was the reason why strict schedules had to be worked out.

Soon, everyone discovered that living together was going to be extremely difficult. Week after week, they were shut in. Never could they step out-of-doors. It was as if they were in a prison, without guards.

Each of them was given chores to do. Naturally, there was the cleaning and cooking. The three young people also had to continue with their school lessons. They kept busy reading and studying. Finally, everyone did office work—such as filing, accounting, and writing letters. This was done to repay the courageous Dutch people who were risking their lives to help them.

Summer ended. The weather turned chilly. The trees along the Prinsengracht lost their leaves. In November, another person moved in. He was a dentist, named Albert Dussel. Now there were eight of them crowded into the small apartment.

Getting along together became ever harder. The space was so little. The atmosphere was always

tense. Even under the best of conditions, life would have been difficult. But these were not good conditions. Quite the opposite, they were the worst. They had to make sure that nobody working in the building heard them. There was the constant fear that they would be discovered. This only added to their nervousness.

The families in hiding were not able to leave the apartment. But they certainly were not cut off from the outside world. For example, they owned a radio. At night, they listened eagerly to the war news. Every so often there was some hopeful development. For a little while, they would feel cheerful.

In the evenings, Anne was free to do as she pleased. She would amuse herself by staring out the window. Sometimes, she saw birds fly by. When night had fallen and the lights of the city were out, she used her telescope. In this way, she could spy on the world outside.

In spite of the war and the horrible suffering taking place, the seasons changed as usual. In the spring, roses bloomed in the street below. The lovely weather made Anne feel incredibly restless.

She exclaimed to Peter, "Oh, if only I could run in the street and breathe some fresh air!"

Peter said nothing. He seldom did. Mostly, he was a silent, teenage boy. From the beginning, Anne had not been greatly impressed by him.

"Peter, come here," she called. "See how beautiful the roofs look. Wouldn't you like to ride your bicycle? Or dance? I would." Anne yearned to feel free. She hated having to breathe fresh air through a little crack in the window. It made her feel like crying.

Peter nodded sympathetically. But he could think of nothing comforting to say.

Anne and Peter were usually bored listening to the conversations of the adults. All their parents ever seemed to do was complain. They fussed about everything from food to politics. They were quick to notice any mistakes the youngsters made.

Anne couldn't stand their nagging. She especially resented it when her parents compared her to Margot.

"Margot really is perfect, isn't she?" Anne said to Peter. "She's quiet, tidy, pretty, busy. She doesn't have one single fault."

Peter could not help laughing. "You wouldn't be jealous, would you?" he replied.

Anne loved her sister. It was not jealousy. But she was fed up at the way her parents always scolded her.

During the months in hiding, Anne had begun to change. She was still thoughtful and quick to criticize herself. But now, she was also growing up. Like any adolescent going through the normal changes of the teenage years, Anne felt unsure of

herself. She needed to find out who she was. Often, this need drew her into battles with her parents.

Now, more of her time was spent daydreaming. She let out her deepest feelings by writing in her diary. Day after day, she kept a record of her thoughts and the things that went on in the household.

As time went on, she grew closer to Peter. Now, he seemed friendlier. He, too, had begun to argue a lot with his parents. Peter had the most trouble with his mother. Anne could certainly understand why. In her opinion, Mrs. Van Daan was a spoiled, silly woman.

One day, Anne asked him, "What will you do when the war is over?"

"Live on a plantation in the Dutch East Indies. What about you?"

"I want to be a writer," Anne said. "But first I'll have to study hard."

It struck Anne that she enjoyed talking to Peter. They were always fighting with the grown-ups and often feeling sad. But when the war was over, their lives would be different. They should be friends and help each other. Both of them needed someone to talk to.

"Why don't we study together?" she suggested. "Maybe we could discuss things."

"I'd like that very much," Peter said, squeezing her hand. Anne was happy to have a friend.

Loss of freedom was awful. Loneliness and fear of discovery were hideous. But perhaps the most unbearable part of hiding was putting up with small daily annoyances. The tiniest things could spark a quarrel. Cut off from the world, always fearful of capture, they had to depend on their friends for everything. If Miep and the others were ever caught, they would face terrible punishments. Knowing that didn't help the refugees.

Many arguments broke out over food. It was one of their biggest problems. Of course, survival depended on food. Before hiding, Mr. Frank and Mr. Van Daan had bought large quantities of provisions. There were sacks of beans and potatoes, cans of vegetables, even some preserved meat.

But by 1943, the war showed no sign of ending. They had not counted on this. Even though they ate sparingly, their supplies were running low. Luckily, their friends were able to get extra food stamps and bring them fresh food.

To keep life simple, the kitchen was run on an unusual system. For long stretches, their meals would consist of only one or two foods. For example, they might eat potatoes and beets for two weeks. At other periods, there was only spinach—or turnips—or cabbage. Day after day, they had the same thing for both lunch and dinner. Sometimes, the food would be cooked in a different way.

But often, it was cooked the same. When this happened, there would be complaints. Tempers snapped. There were ugly scenes at the table. Everyone would begin quarreling.

The only person who never joined in the bickering was Margot. She took no interest in food and ate little.

On the other hand, Mrs. Van Daan was always in the middle of a fight. "Vegetables are good for you," she would insist. "Margot is too pale. She doesn't eat enough."

Mrs. Van Daan always annoyed Anne. Hearing her talking about Margot, Anne said, "At least she doesn't waste food. Some people here eat more than their fair share."

"What impertinence!" Mrs. Van Daan burst out. "Are you accusing me?"

Most of the arguments were pointless. But they could also get nasty. Afterwards, there would be hurt feelings on everyone's part.

Anne was irritated by both Mrs. Van Daan and her husband. They were nosy and bossy. Mr. Van Daan simply could not keep his mouth shut. Talking constantly, he pretended to know everything. At meals, his wife gave him favored treatment. Not only was he served first, but he also got the best bits of food.

In addition, Mrs. Van Daan never missed a chance to show off her knowledge. She was a lively

woman with a good deal of charm. But she was also a great gossip. It gave her pleasure to stir up trouble between Anne and her mother.

Mr. and Mrs. Van Daan did have their good points, however. Neither of them were gloomy individuals. When they weren't busy fighting, they managed to create a cheerful atmosphere.

To avoid being heard by the office workers below, the refugees had to follow a strict schedule. Breakfast—dry bread and margarine—was at nine o'clock. Lunch was at one. They ate supper after the workers had gone home for the day.

Evening was the time to relax. Friends visited. Miep, Elli Vossen, Mr. Kraler, and Mr. Koophuis often joined them for supper. Afterwards, they would gather around the radio, listening to news broadcasts from the British Broadcasting Corporation.

Life in the apartment was not all gloom and fear. Although there were tensions, they had happy times as well. On such occasions, everybody smiled and behaved pleasantly. For a little while, they forgot their troubles. There was always one person who would say, "Someday we'll look back on this time...."

Anne was not only the youngest member of the group, but also the merriest. Peeling potatoes or shelling peas, she always managed to make jokes. She had a rich imagination. Somehow, she found

ways to keep from getting bored. One way she amused herself was by dancing. It also was good exercise.

Over the months, there were frequent celebrations. Religious holidays were observed. Birthdays and anniversaries were remembered with cards, poems, and small gifts. For her mother's birthday, Anne created a special ballet. She made a costume out of an old petticoat and decorated it with colorful ribbons. Mr. Kraler even managed to find them some sugar. So they were able to bake a splendid cake.

Mrs. Frank's birthday party turned out to be an especially festive occasion. Mrs. Van Daan was very envious.

Another year passed. It was 1944. They had been in hiding for nineteen months. By now, Anne's problems with her family had grown worse. Relations with her mother were particularly bad. Sometimes, she said harsh things that hurt her mother. Mrs. Frank cried. Anne made a promise to herself. If she could help it, she would never become like her mother.

"If God lets me live through this," she decided, "I'll do things she has never done. I'll never be ordinary the way she is."

Mr. Frank and Margot begged Anne to try and understand her mother. They reminded her that Mrs. Frank had been born into a wealthy family.

She had never been accustomed to hardship. Making sacrifices and living from hand-to-mouth had changed her. How could Anne expect the poor woman to be happy and easygoing?

Anne's father was a kind man. But he couldn't give her the things she needed. Nobody could. For all three of the youngsters, life was becoming unbearable. They needed to break away from their families and meet new people. To develop independence, they had to go out into the world and have experiences. All of these things were impossible in hiding.

Sometimes, Anne loved everyone in the apartment. But just as often, she felt lonely. It seemed as if nobody understood her. Nobody treated her fairly. Quarreling with her parents was bad enough. But she also fought with Mr. Dussel. She found him disagreeable. He was quick to point out her faults.

In her diary, Anne wrote, "I realize that when I came here, in 1942, I was an impertinent, spoiled little girl, sincere but not realistic. That time is over now." She longed for the day when the war would end. Then, life would be good again.

On Easter Sunday, 1944, a terrifying incident took place. About 9:30 that evening, Peter was studying. Suddenly, he heard an unusual sound. Downstairs, on the street, someone was trying to force open the door to the warehouse. This was not

the first time that Kohlen and Company had been visited by burglars. Each break-in had made them more tense and jumpy than ever.

Peter did not want to alarm everyone. He notified Mr. Frank. Immediately, all the lights were turned off. The girls and their mother were sent upstairs to the Van Daans. The men waited to hear what would happen next. Soon, there was a loud crash.

The men rushed downstairs. The burglars had smashed a panel on the storeroom door. They were busy trying to widen the hole and squeeze into the storeroom.

"Police!" Mr. Van Daan cried, at the top of his voice. "Police!"

The burglars ran away. Mr. Frank and the other men hurried to replace the panel on the front door. At that very moment, however, a man and a woman came walking down the street. Hearing the commotion, they hurried over to find out what was going on. They saw the hole in the door. Pulling out a flashlight, they inspected the damage. Then they walked away.

"They will certainly call the police," Peter worried aloud.

Everyone showed their fear in a variety of ways. How could they escape the Nazis now? All Mrs.Van Daan could think about was hiding the

radio. Mrs. Frank was worried about Anne's diary. She wanted to burn it.

"Nonsense," Mr. Frank interrupted. "If they find us, the fact that we're Jewish is enough. Now let's try to be brave."

All that night, the eight refugees hid in the darkness. They waited for the Nazi secret police to break down the door. But the Gestapo did not come.

At seven the next morning, someone went down to the office and telephoned Mr. Koophuis. It was important to let their friends know what had taken place.

Miep and her husband Henk arrived at the building. To explain their presence on a holiday, they said they had come to feed the warehouse cat. The refugees found out that the night watchman had called the police. But when the authorities arrived, they were told that there was no need to search the warehouse. The burglars had fled. Nothing had been stolen.

The couple who had passed by were a fruit seller and his wife. They lived in the neighborhood. Miep said that she would not be surprised if the couple already suspected.

"We're sure they won't talk," Miep said.

Afterwards, everyone felt exhausted. The memory of that frightening night stayed with Anne for a long time.

Looking to the Future

The weather was warm and sunny. It was one of those glorious days when everyone wants to be outside. Of course, none of the refugees could go out-of-doors and enjoy the fine day. All they could do was use their imaginations. What might they have done had the situation been different? Days like this one were especially difficult.

"When will we ever be able to do as we please?" Anne asked her father.

"The news is good," he said. Many countries had joined together to fight Germany. "The Allies are making progress. Soon, the war will be over."

"Maybe so," said Mr. Van Daan. But he worried that hatred of the Jews was spreading. "People blame us for everything," he added bitterly.

Mr. Frank thought the Nazis were to blame. They punished anyone who tried to protect the Jews.

Anne could not help wondering what would happen when they finally left the hideaway. When the Franks had first arrived from Germany, years ago, the Dutch had welcomed them. But ever since the Nazi occupation, many Dutch people had turned their backs on the Jews. When the war ended, would

the Dutch throw them out? Anne had grown up in Holland. It was more a home to her than Germany. Mr. Frank tried to cheer her up. Trying to guess what the future held was too depressing. It would be better to think about peace and all the good things it would bring.

Peter, too, was eager to change the subject. "What would you all like to do when we get out of here?" he asked.

Margot was the first to answer. "Have a real bath with hot water!" she burst out.

"Me too!" added Mrs. Van Daan. "A long bath."

"I'm going to look for my wife Lotte," said Mr. Dussel sadly.

Finally, it was Anne's turn. She had so many dreams that it was impossible to choose just one. "I want to live in my own house," she said. "I want my freedom back, and I want to be able to return to my old school and see all my friends." It made no difference what her religion was, she said. Wasn't she young? Why shouldn't she have a chance to be happy and have fun? She dreamed of leading a normal life.

Her words touched Mrs. Van Daan. She looked at Anne with tears in her eyes. "You're right, my dear," she said. "Soon this nightmare will be over. The Allies will invade Europe. Then, we can leave here and go back to our old lives."

But her husband disagreed. Soon, they were bickering as always. Everyone tried to ignore them. Peter went over to Anne, who could not stop talking. She could see herself traveling to Paris or London. Maybe she would study art history or languages. Perhaps she would write a book about everything that happened to her during the war. She definitely planned to be famous someday.

"I almost envy you," said Peter. "You have so many dreams."

Anne looked surprised. "Envy me? Why? Don't you ever dream? Why should I let myself get sad and lose hope for the future?" So many bad things had happened. But she *still* believed that there are good people in the world. Nature was beautiful. And each day freedom was getting closer.

Peter smiled in admiration. "Oh, Anne," he said, "how brave and strong you are. I wish we all could feel more like you."

That evening, they heard the sound of air raid sirens. The sirens meant that Allied aircraft were heading their way. Soon, bombs would come raining down. The people of Amsterdam rushed to take cover. Many people hid in air raid shelters. But the eight refugees could not leave their hiding place.

They held their breath, hoping that the siren was only a false alarm. But the roar of the planes overhead grew louder and louder. They knew that

the bombing was about to begin. All they could do was pray that the building would not be hit.

The racket was deafening. On the ground, the antiaircraft guns began to fire at the planes. The noise of the guns mingled with the sounds of bombs exploding. The bombardment was the most terrifying sound imaginable. The falling bombs made whistling sounds. Then came the roar and vibration of the explosion, when a bomb hit the ground.

The sky darkened. Houses trembled. Windows shattered into thousands of pieces. Burning buildings threw fiery tongues of flame into the air.

What would happen to them if a bomb landed on their building? Where would they go?

Anne was deathly afraid of the bombing. It made her want to scream out loud in fear. She clung to her parents. Mr. and Mrs. Frank held her. They tried to comfort her as best they could.

Her heart beat wildly. "Daddy, light a candle!" she begged. "Please, light a candle."

"You know I can't. Please try and be brave."

"I feel so afraid in the dark!"

Finally, Mrs. Frank took pity on her daughter. She ran to light a candle. Anne sat up, clutching her little suitcase. If a bomb hit, she was ready to flee.

Anne was not the only one who feared the bombs. All of them felt the same. Nobody tried to hide their feelings, for this was truly a nightmare.

By the middle of July 1944, much of Amsterdam lay in ruins. Countless people had died. The hospitals were filled with wounded. Survivors wandered around the smoking ruins. They scarcely knew what was going on around them.

Another terrible day of bombing took place at the end of July. The first alarm shrieked during breakfast. A second alarm sounded at around two o'clock. Still another warning came in the evening, at dinnertime. Just as Amsterdam was recovering from one wave of terror, the sirens announced the next one on its way.

The sky was crowded with planes. Engines screaming, the aircraft unloaded tons of bombs on the city. In the glare of the flames, Amsterdam looked like a mass of holes and craters.

Everyone in the apartment felt desperately tired. Several weeks earlier, they had heard a chilling story. The Nazis had arrested a man who owned the fruit and vegetable market just up the street. He had been hiding two Jews in his home. This was terribly frightening to Anne and the others. It gave them even more to worry about. Ever

since the arrest, they were in constant fear for both themselves and their protectors.

The last two years had been long and dangerous for Miep, Mr. Kraler, and Mr. Koophuis. Taking care of eight refugees required a great deal of their time and energy.

The hottest part of the summer had arrived. Food was scarce. Much of what they did obtain was rotten. Sewers were blocked; all because of damage caused by the bombing. Even the water was not fit to drink.

These days, everyone seemed more nervous than usual. It was not only fatigue and hunger and fear of capture. They also felt as if *something* was about to happen. All of them became aware of the feeling. It hung in the air. Moods changed like lightning. The tension mounted.

Suddenly, they thought they could hear unusual noises. It sounded as if someone was walking around in the warehouse. Had their apartment been discovered? Or was someone only suspicious—only snooping around to see if there was a secret hiding place?

One evening, around midnight, they heard the noise again.

"There's someone there!" Mr. Frank said. "I'm sure of it."

Upstairs, the Van Daans heard the same disturbing sounds.

Although it was time for bed, sleep became impossible. Throughout the night, the slightest noise got them up. They listened anxiously. There was no doubt about it. Someone was hanging around on the landing, near the bookcase that led to the apartment. Everyone had the same thought. "Who could be poking around out there?"

Whoever it was, he or she was someone who hated Jews. The Gestapo paid money to anyone who gave information that led to an arrest. An informer could earn five gulden (about $1.40) for each Jew reported to the secret police.

For two years, Miep and Elli and their other friends had been very careful. But lately, they had become aware of someone giving them suspicious glances. It was one of the men who worked in the storeroom. He seemed to be unusually interested in their comings and goings.

"He's always hanging around on the street," Elli noticed. "Sometimes I see him near the entrance to the warehouse. But whenever I look at him, he pretends to be fixing his bicycle."

"Yes," Mr. Kraler agreed. "He certainly seems very curious. And that man is no fool. I don't trust him at all."

Miep sighed. "It's no surprise," she said. "The war has changed everyone. Even children have learned how to hate. People only think of themselves now, even if it means doing harm to others."

“We Must Be *Strong;* We Must *Never* Give In”

One morning, Anne woke as usual at a quarter-past-seven. Everyone in the apartment began getting up. One by one, they took turns washing. Down in the street, the city was coming to life. The sounds of traffic and people hurrying to work could be heard.

The date was August 4, 1944. Two months earlier, Allied forces had landed on the beaches of Normandy, in France. "D-day"—the invasion of Europe—had lifted the spirits of everyone in the hideaway.

On the pavement outside Kohlen and Company stood a man about forty years old. He was smoking a cigar. Every so often, he peered up and down the street. It was clear that he was waiting for someone.

Soon, four men in raincoats came walking along Prinsengracht Canal. When they reached Kohlen and Company, the man with the cigar went up to them. He was nodding. “This is the place,” he said. Together the men entered the building. Mr. Kraler was working in his office.

"I'm a Gestapo officer," one of the men announced.

"We wish to search the warehouse," said another. Like his companions, he was dressed in the uniform of the Dutch Nazi Police. He carried a gun.

Mr. Kraler began showing the Gestapo officers around the building. They looked closely at everything. When nothing remained to be seen, Mr. Kraler began to relax a little. He hoped that the Nazis would leave now.

But then the officers headed straight for the entrance to the secret apartment. When they reached the revolving bookcase, they stopped.

"Open it!" their leader ordered Mr. Kraler.

"But it's just a bookcase," Mr. Kraler protested. "How can I open it?"

Mr. Kraler was shoved aside. With pistols drawn, the men began to wrench at the bookcase. In a moment, it turned on its hinges. There was the hidden door.

A gun was pushed into Mr. Kraler's back. He was forced to lead the Nazis up the stairs.

Mrs. Frank was sitting at a table. She watched helplessly as Mr. Kraler and the Germans climbed the steps. The others living in the hideaway came to join her. Everyone stood in a line.

"Hands up!" an officer snapped.

Nobody spoke. Then the stunned refugees lifted their arms. The Nazis began to search the

rooms. Clothing and papers were scattered all over the floor.

The chief officer looked pleased. It had not been a false alarm, after all. The man with the cigar had known exactly what he was talking about.

The officer told the refugees, "You're coming with us. You have five minutes to pack."

Anne stuffed a few things into her school bag. Only clothing could be taken. Everything else had to be left behind, even her diary.

Anne could not believe this was happening. Their worst fears had come true. Countless times, they had talked about being arrested and imprisoned in a concentration camp. And yet, Anne had always felt optimistic. In her mind, she refused to admit that such a terrible thing could happen.

The prisoners were taken to Westerbork, a large concentration camp in Holland. Conditions in the camp were bad. Masses of people were crowded together. There were no washbasins and few toilets. The prisoners were stripped of their clothing. They had to wear blue uniforms and wooden shoes. Then, they were assigned to various barracks. In each small building lived three hundred inmates.

Among all those people, the eight friends stood out. Their faces looked sickly white. For two years, they had never gone out into the sunshine.

What would happen to them now? They had fallen into the hands of evil forces who meant to

destroy all Jews. Their fates depended on the hateful Nazis.

Mr. Frank did his best to be encouraging. "We mustn't lose the strength to fight," he urged.

The days were long. Each morning, they were awakened at five A.M. The work they were forced to do was very hard. Food was scarce—and bad.

Anne and Peter stuck together. They helped each other and found comfort in their friendship. But Anne's mother became terribly depressed. She seldom spoke. Nobody could make her snap out of her depressed mood.

Meanwhile, the war had taken a new turn. Around the camp flew rumors that Paris had been freed on August 25. Hopes of survival were rekindled!

On September 3, the Allies were drawing closer to the camp. The city of Brussels, Belgium, was captured. On that same day, however, a thousand Jews were chosen to leave Westerbork. Among the group were the Franks and their friends.

They were forced to board a long freight train. Seventy-five people were crammed into each car. There was no air, little water, and only a little black bread. For three days and nights, the train jerked along. They did not know where they were going or how long it would take.

On the third night, the train stopped. The doors were thrown open. Voices of SS men rang out.

"Come on, out!" Hurry!" Yelling commands, the SS guards ran up and down the platform. They kept their eyes on the Jews leaving the cars.

The journey had left the prisoners weak and hungry. Where were they? The night was pitch black. A few floodlights lit the train platform. Then a whisper passed through the crowd. It was the dreaded name—Auschwitz—the terrible concentration camp in Poland. A chill of fear ran over everyone. They waited in silence. The only sounds were the harsh voices of the guards and the barking of dogs.

Suddenly, a loudspeaker began to blare. "Men to the right, women to the left," a voice commanded.

There was no time—even to say good-bye. They were pushed forward like parts of a machine. The women had to file off in one direction; the men were herded in another. Anne turned to say good-bye to her father and Peter. But it was too late...they had already been carried off into the darkness. Anne squeezed Margot's hand. Their mother looked dazed.

Weary and frightened, the women walked along in the dark. After a while, they reached Block 29 and the barracks where they were to live.

Soon, Anne came to know the camp at Auschwitz-Birkenau. It was surrounded by a barbed-wire fence, which had been electrified. In tall towers, sentries with machine guns kept watch over the prisoners, day and night. At the main entrance

to the camp was a sign. It read "ARBEIT MACHT FREI"—WORK WILL MAKE YOU FREE. Row after row of brick barracks became home to groups of Poles, Jews, Gypsies, and Russians.

When Anne and her family arrived at the camp, they were greeted by a German officer. His welcome was a horrible warning. "You have not come to a hospital," the officer told new arrivals. "This is a German concentration camp. You will never leave, except as smoke from the chimney." And he added, "If you don't like it, you'd better throw yourselves against the electrified fence."

The camp commander, Rudolf Hess, had turned Auschwitz into a "model" camp. The murder of prisoners had been carefully organized. The death program consisted of work, starvation, a variety of punishments, and then—death by gassing.

Anne's few belongings were taken away from her. She no longer owned any possessions. She was given an identifying number—which was painfully and permanently tattooed on her arm. Most of her hair was shaved off. A gray, sack-like gown became her only clothing. To identify her as a Jew, a yellow strip of cloth, in the shape of a triangle, was sewn on the garment. Already thin, Anne seemed even younger than her fifteen years.

At first, Anne felt tremendous relief, because she had not been separated from her mother and sister. But after a while, she realized that it was

ARBEIT MACHT

only another form of cruelty. Watching each other's suffering made things far worse.

Still, Anne tried to remain cheerful. Somehow, she was able to smile. Whenever she could, she tried to comfort her mother.

"Someday this will all end, Mother," she said. "You'll see. We'll get out of here."

Secretly, she went around the camp and searched for things that could be of help to Mrs. Frank. She would bring back a piece of cloth or some fresh water.

"Drink, Mother, drink," she coaxed. Anne bent down and helped her, as if her mother were a child.

Mrs. Frank refused. "I've had some," she would reply. "You drink."

Anne saw that her mother was giving up. Her physical and mental strength were fading. Margot, too, seemed to be getting weaker and child-like.

"We must be *strong*; we must *never* give in!" Anne told them. "Remember what Daddy said? 'We mustn't lose the strength to fight.' "

One wet day, Anne noticed a group of Hungarian children sitting in the rain. They were waiting their turn to enter the gas chambers. Looking into their eyes, she burst into tears.

"It's not fair! It's not fair!"

Anne longed to save them. But she could do nothing except weep at their terrible fate.

From One Corner of Hell to Another

The pain and horror of the concentration camps can never be undone. People suffered in the worst ways that the human mind could invent. There were exhausting marches in the freezing cold and rain. Day or night, roll call would be taken. People would be forced to stand for hours at a time. Many prisoners starved to death. Punishment and torture were common.

Every day, men, women, and children were put to death in the gas chambers. Mothers tried in vain to hide their children. But even the tiniest babies were killed. Their bodies were loaded onto a belt and carried into the crematorium. There, they were burned. The air was foul with the smell of burning flesh. All of the prisoners had to live with the smell of this smoke.

Auschwitz was known for its inhuman punishments. At evening roll call, prisoners were beaten with a leather whip. It was supposed to be an example for those who had to watch. Another form of punishment was standing at attention for hours. The "Stehzelle" were tiny cells, like a dog kennel. The victim was forced to stand up all the time, without food or water.

Sometimes, the only way to escape these horrors was to choose death. People would kill themselves on the electrified fence or be gunned down by the guards.

Anne refused to give in. She struggled to be strong and comfort those around her. Most painful of all was seeing her mother so depressed and ill.

"Poor Mother," she often said to Margot. "There is nothing we can do to help her."

Two months passed. One evening in October came disturbing news. The youngest and strongest prisoners were being transferred to yet another camp—Bergen-Belsen, in Germany.

The guards made the women line up outside their barracks. Some of the women straightened their clothes and tidied their hair. They wanted to hide any signs of weakness or tiredness. Those who appeared ill, old, or weak would be rejected. Being rejected might mean they would be the next ones sent to die in the gas chambers.

One by one, the women were made to walk under a spotlight. The guards looked at them carefully. As Anne and Margot passed by, they heard a voice say, "This one, yes. This one, yes."

Relieved, Anne and Margot were sent to stand in another line. They waited for their mother to join them. Instead, the guard said, "This one, no."

Mrs. Frank could not hide her panic. "For the love of God, not my children!" she cried. "Don't take

my children from me!"

The girls and their mother were barely able to touch hands one last time. Then they were torn from each other—forever—by the vicious Nazi soldiers.

The journey to Bergen-Belsen took a long time. Anne and Margot could not speak—all of their hope for the future had fled.

Bergen-Belsen was in northern Germany. The camp was run by Joseph Kramer, who had come from Auschwitz. There were no gas chambers at this camp, and it lacked the organization of Auschwitz. But prisoners died by the thousands, just the same. Their deaths were caused by starvation and disease. One of the most common illnesses in the camp was typhus, which was caused by lack of sanitation and clean water.

Everywhere was the most hideous filth. The barracks were full of ill, starving, and dying people. Outside lay a pile of dead bodies. The corpses were barely covered with a sprinkling of earth and lime. The smell of rotting flesh was sickening.

The sight of such human misery was truly shocking. Anne and Margot clung to each other's hands. They tried to give each other courage. But both of them realized that survival would be even more difficult in this place.

There were no predictable meal calls at Bergen-Belsen. Food was not distributed regularly. It was like being thrust into hell.

Margot looked around at the vast number of graves. Starving the prisoners to death was just another method of murder, she decided.

Soon after their arrival, Anne learned that one of her school friends was also there. One day, she received a message from Lies Goosens. The two girls arranged to meet. Lies was living in another block. But—if they were careful—they could find a way to see each other in the evening. They planned to meet at a fence.

Anne felt overjoyed. Once, Lies Goosens had been one of her dearest friends.

That evening, it was dark when Anne left the barracks. An icy wind began to blow. But she managed to find the place. Very quietly she called out to her old friend, "Lies! Lies! Where are you?"

Then she heard Lies's voice. "Anne, I'm right over here."

Although they recognized each other immediately, the two girls stared at each other. Their suffering in the camps had changed their appearances greatly. Both looked extremely thin and pale in a very unhealthy way.

Through the barbed wire, they talked in whispers. They spoke of themselves and their families. How unreal the Montessori School seemed to them, now. They began to cry over the incredible things that had happened to them.

Soon, it was time to part and return to their blocks. Lies had something for Anne. It was a package she had received from the Red Cross. She wanted to share some of the little luxuries with her friend. There was a sweater, a biscuit, and a little sugar. Lies threw the package over the fence.

Anne lifted her thin arms. She stood on her tiptoes. Just then, another prisoner rushed up and meanly ripped the parcel from her hand. After a struggle, the woman ran away. Anne began to cry.

The winter of 1945 was severe. Hunger and thirst made life unbearable. Many of the prisoners resigned themselves to death. Others tried to survive by any means possible. Like the woman who snatched Anne's package, they stole. The prisoners with weaker consciences failed to respect their fellow victims. Sadly, those prisoners who arrived without strong moral values became like their jailers. For them, all signs of love or ordinary human goodness had vanished.

Margot became seriously ill. Each day, she grew thinner. She looked ghostly white. All her energy had drained away. Anne scoured the camp, searching for someone who might help her sister.

But in that wretched place, nobody answered her plea for help. There were no toilets. The buildings were filthy. Typhus was raging.

By February, Margot could no longer follow what Anne said. She was too weak to concentrate.

The deadly typhus fevers were doing the dirty-work for the Nazis.

The camp was affecting Anne's health, too. She began to have dreams that carried her backward in time. These dreams blotted out the images and smells of the barracks. Suddenly, she would be back in Amsterdam with her mother and father and Peter. She watched herself at school, laughing with her friends. Or, at other times, she was simply sitting at home, talking with Margot.

Suddenly, the dream changed. The air was filled with a foul smell. Anne woke up with a start. She realized that the stench of the barracks had disturbed her happy dream.

Never Forget! It Must Never Happen Again

Anne never dreamed about the hideaway. Perhaps that was because she often thought about the apartment while she was awake. She wondered about many things. Was her mother still alive? Where were her father and Peter now?

"They would help me to have the courage to go on," she thought. "Oh, if *only* I knew what has happened to Peter!"

Thinking about him took her back to the days in hiding. They weren't such bad times after all, she decided. She had been able to read and study. In spite of everything, they had had happy moments.

"If only we could all still be there together," she wished, "waiting for peace to come."

Sometimes, she felt *so* tired. She would throw herself down on her bed, scarcely able to move. She felt *almost* as if she wanted to die. But then, she would scold herself. She *knew* that she had to stay alive for the sake of her loved ones.

She *willed* herself to live. People all over the world must know about the suffering they had experienced. Then, no one would ever be able to forget what had happened. Usually such thoughts made her feel stronger.

Despite her determination, Anne was unable to overcome the horrors of Bergen-Belsen. In March 1945, her sister died. Now...she was alone. A few days after Margot's death, Anne also died.

...Two months later, the war came to an end.

The Wonder of Life

ermany was defeated in the spring of 1945. Peace came to Europe. All along, the Nazis had planned to destroy the concentration camps if Germany lost the war. They were going to kill any prisoners who were still alive. It was important to hide evidence of their cruelty. Then the world would never have to know about the horrors that had taken place in the death camps.

But the Allied armies had moved too quickly. The Nazis were taken by surprise. Their plans to destroy the camps were only partly carried out.

In 1945, the gates of camps like Auschwitz and Bergen-Belsen were thrown open. For the first time, the world learned that *millions* of victims had died. And they learned how—for there stood the cells and the ovens. The mass graves could not be hidden. Wherever one looked, the evidence was obvious. The Nazis had devised the most terrifying methods of torture that anyone could remember.

Earlier in the year, the sounds of Russian guns began to echo through the Polish countryside. At Auschwitz, the SS heard rumors that Russian troops might free the prisoners. It was decided that 11,000 must be moved immediately. In wintry January, they were made to march, on foot, to other German death camps.

At that time, Otto Frank was in the Auschwitz hospital. He did not accompany the others, who nearly all died of fatigue, hunger, or cold. The reason he had been left behind was simple: nobody remembered his existence.

Russian soldiers entering Auschwitz gave Mr. Frank his liberty. But he was not able to return to Holland at once. First, he was transported to the Polish town of Kattowicze, and from there to Odessa, in the Soviet Union. It was quite a while before he could go back to Holland.

Eight people had shared the secret apartment. The only one to survive was Otto Frank. The rest died in the concentration camps or simply disappeared.

When Mr. Frank returned to Amsterdam, he met the Dutch friends who had helped his family. A joyous reunion took place with Mr. Kraler, Mr. Koophuis, Miep, and Elli. They had much to talk about.

Mr. Frank was overcome with emotion. "How often I thought about all of you," he said. "You risked death by helping us."

His friends assured him that they had no regrets about what they had done.

Elli said, "We have something that we've been saving for you."

During the arrest, the Gestapo had searched the apartment. Papers had been scattered

everywhere. "We found this after you had gone," Miep said. She handed Mr. Frank a book.

Mr. Frank was stunned. "It's Anne's diary!" he exclaimed. "It's my little girl's diary. I can't believe it!"

He held the precious little book, remembering how much it had meant to Anne. Emotions and memories churned inside him. He could think of no words to express his feelings.

Later, when Mr. Frank was alone, he took out the diary. He did not want to invade his daughter's privacy. Her secret feelings should not be exposed. But he needed to be with Anne again. He longed to remember her as she once was. That was the reason why he finally opened the book. He began to read.

On the first page, Anne had written:

"I hope that I will be able to confide in you as I never confided in anyone else, and I hope that you will be a great strength to me. Anne Frank. June 12, 1942."

Those words were priceless to Mr. Frank. Hugging the book to his chest, he felt immensely grateful that the diary had been saved. He continued to thumb through the book. He read a passage here and a passage there.

Anne had written down things about herself and her feelings. For example, there were many remarks about how hard it was to get along with the adults. But she also had written a great deal more.

She described their daily life together in the secret hiding place. She wrote about the food, the burglars, the quarreling Van Daans, and Mr. Dussel the dentist. Here was a record of everyone and everything.

"Yesterday evening," wrote Anne, "there was a short circuit, and the shooting went on and on outside. I thought it would never end. I can never get over my fear of the shooting and the roar of the planes flying overhead, dropping bombs and making the earth shake so. I creep into father's bed nearly every night for comfort. I suppose it's very childish of me, but it makes me feel so much safer."

Her father had been frightened, too. But he had tried to appear brave, and comfort Anne.

Some of Anne's comments caused him to smile. "Spinach and salad for fourteen days now. Sweet potatoes ten inches long that taste moldy. Things have come to a pretty pass..."

He could almost hear her laughing about her ragged clothing. Eventually, her slippers had become threadbare. She had grown out of her skirts. Her blouses were so short that they barely covered her tummy.

It was too painful to read the diary entries in order. Instead, Mr. Frank jumped backwards and forwards over the months.

Anne spoke to the diary as if it were her friend. "The poetry Daddy wrote for me on my

birthday is so beautiful that I'm not going to share it with you."

Mr. Frank stopped to reflect. Anne was fourteen when she wrote that. He remembered her happiness whenever she received a poem or a book about Roman and Greek myths.

Anne's writing stirred so many memories. Mr. Frank felt like weeping. He moved ahead to the last page.

"I know exactly what I would like to be and what I am inside, but alas, I am like that only with myself!"

Mr. Frank could not help thinking, "Not any more. Now everyone will know who you are, my little Anne!"

On May 22, 1944, Anne had written about her adopted country. "I love Holland," she wrote. "I once hoped, and I still do, that Holland can be a homeland for me, a person without a country. Even though I was born in Germany, I have lived in this country so long that it has become more a home to me than my real homeland."

After the war, her hope was to come true. Otto Frank decided to make his home in Amsterdam. He spent the rest of his life working to make sure that the bad treatment of the Jews would not be forgotten.

The Queen of the Netherlands met Anne's father. She was eager to honor him. In this way,

Holland would be able to recognize the young girl who had made known the dramatic plight of the Jews. It also was a way to remember the war years when Holland had been occupied and humiliated by invaders.

Anne had also written in her diary, "I want to live on after I have died. I am glad, then, that God has given me the desire to write down everything about myself...I must, I must, I must..."

After reading the diary, Mr. Frank felt determined to fulfill Anne's wish. He and his friends arranged to have the diary published.

In June 1947, the diary was first printed by Contact Publishers, in Amsterdam. It was titled *The Secret Annexe.*

No matter who had written the diary, it would have been important. It was a real account of the daily life and worries of a Jew living in a Nazi-occupied country. But Anne's diary was even more special because it had been written by a young girl.

The diary became famous throughout the world. The book sold millions of copies. Over the years, it has been translated into dozens of languages, including Chinese and Arabic. There also was a stage play and a movie based on the diary.

Today, Anne Frank's name is remembered everywhere. Just as she had wished, she did become a famous writer. Millions of readers have wept over the story of her family's fate at the hands of the

Nazis. People continue to feel deeply, whenever they read her messages about peace and humanity.

After the war, much of Amsterdam was rebuilt. But the city made a promise to Otto Frank. The building in which Anne and the others had lived would not be changed. What's more, the secret hiding place was to remain exactly as it had been during the war. It would serve as a permanent reminder.

Eventually, Number 263 on the Prinsengracht was completely restored. Today, it is a museum run by the Anne Frank Foundation. The main goal of the foundation is to continue Anne's struggle for peace in the world.

Visitors to the museum find that the hiding place looks exactly as Anne described. The stairways still lead up to the dark old rooms. The furniture is clumsy. The carpets look faded. The stove where they cooked their food is there. So is Anne's tiny room.

A visit there is an extremely moving experience. The outside world seems to fade away. People find themselves left alone with the memory of Anne.

It is impossible to forget that tragic August day when the refugees were discovered. But above all else, there remain the thoughts of a young girl. Even though she grew up with suffering, she taught the world something about the wonder of life.

The Secret Hiding Place

The building of Kohlen & Co. is located at No. 263 on the Prinsengracht Canal in Amsterdam. On the ground floor is a large warehouse with the offices located on the first floor. The secret rooms where the eight refugees lived are on the second and third floors. A wooden staircase led from the first-floor corridor to the second-floor landing where there were two doors. The one on the left led to the street, storeroom, and the attics from where a steep staircase led down to the second street door.

The right-hand door led to the internal flat where the hiding place was. No one suspected that so many rooms lay concealed behind an ordinary gray door. Immediately upon entering there was a steep staircase on the right, and on the left a short corridor which led to the bedroom belonging to Anne's parents. A small adjoining room belonged to the Franks' daughters, Anne and Margot. On the right of the staircase there was a small, windowless room with a washbasin and separate toilet. There was a communication door between this room and the sisters' room.

Upon opening the door at the top of the stairs, one was astonished to find such a large, well-lit room in an old house on the canal. There was a gas oven (thanks to the fact that the room had once been a laboratory) and a sink. The room doubled as a kitchen and the Van Daan's bedroom, as well as being the dining room, living room, and work room for all the refugees.

A small hallway became Peter's apartment. Then, finally, as on the street side of the rest of the building, there was an attic.

This model of the secret lodgings can be seen at the Anne Frank Foundation. The Foundation maintains the building at 263 Prinsengracht, where the eight people lived in hiding for two years and one month.

House Rules in the Hideaway

This is a humorous entry from Anne's diary, which she described as a "Prospectus and Guide to the 'Secret Annexe.'"

Open all year round: Beautiful, quiet, free from woodland surroundings, in the heart of Amsterdam. Can be reached by trams 13 and 17, also by car or bicycle. In special cases also on foot, if the Germans prevent the use of transport.

Board and lodging: Free.

Special fat-free diet.

Running water in the bathroom (alas, no bath) and down various inside and outside walls.

Ample storage room for all types of goods.

Own radio center, direct communication with London, New York, Tel Aviv, and numerous other stations. This appliance is only for residents' use after six o'clock in the evening. No stations are forbidden, on the understanding that German stations are only listened to in special cases, such as classical music and the like.

Rest hours: 10 o'clock in the evening until 7:30 in the morning. 10:15 on Sundays. Residents may rest during the day, conditions permitting, as the director indicates. For reasons of public security rest hours must be strictly observed!!

Holidays (outside the home): postponed indefinitely.

Use of language: Speak softly at all times, by order! All civilized languages are permitted, therefore no German!

Lessons: One written shorthand lesson per week. English, French, Mathematics, and History at all times.

Small Pets-Special Department (permit is necessary): Good treatment available (vermin excepted).

Mealtimes: breakfast, every day except Sunday and Bank Holidays, 9 A.M. Sundays and Bank Holidays, 11:30 A.M. approximately.

Lunch (not very big): 1:15 P.M. to 1:45 P.M.

Dinner: cold and/or hot: no fixed time (depending on news broadcast).

Duties: Residents must always be ready to help with office work.

Baths: The washtub is available for all residents from 9 A.M. on Sundays. The W.C. ["water-closet" or toilet], kitchen, private office, or main office, whichever preferred, are available.

Alcoholic Beverages: only with doctor's prescription.

The end.

Letters from Anne's Diary

Monday, 22 May, 1944

. . . To our great horror and regret we hear that the attitude of a great many people towards us Jews has changed. We hear that there is anti-Semitism now in circles that never thought of it before. The news has affected us all very, very deeply. The cause of this hatred of the Jews is understandable, even human sometimes, but not good. The Christians blame the Jews for giving secrets away to the Germans, for betraying their helpers and for the fact that, through the Jews a great many Christians have gone the way of so many others before them, and suffered terrible punishments and a dreadful fate. . .

When one hears this one naturally wonders why we are carrying on with this long and difficult war. We always hear that we're all fighting together for freedom, truth, and right!. . .

Tuesday, 6 June, 1944

Great commotion in the "Secret Annexe!" Would the long awaited liberation that has been talked of so much, but which still seems too wonderful, too much like a fairy tale, ever come true? Could we be granted victory this year, 1944? We don't know yet, but hope is revived within us; it gives us fresh courage, and makes us strong again. Since we must put up bravely with all the fears, privations, and sufferings, the great thing now is to remain calm and steadfast. Now more than ever we must clench our teeth and not cry out. France, Russia, Italy, and Germany, too, can all cry out and give vent to their misery, but we haven't the right to do that yet!. . . Oh, Kitty, the best part of the invasion is that I have the feeling that friends are approaching. We have been oppressed by those terrible Germans for so long, they have had their knives so at our throats, that the thoughts of friends and delivery fills us with confidence!

Thursday, 15 June, 1944

I wonder if it's because I haven't been able to poke my nose outdoors for so long that I've grown so crazy about everything to do with nature? I can perfectly well remember that there was a time when a deep blue sky, the song of the birds, moonlight and flowers could never have kept me spellbound. That's changed since I've been here.

. . . A lot of people are fond of nature, many sleep outdoors occasionally, and people in prisons and hospitals long for the day when they will be free to enjoy the beauties of nature, but few are so shut away and isolated from that which can be shared alike by rich and poor. It's not imagination on my part when I say that to look up at the sky, the clouds, the moon, and the stars makes me calm and patient. . . . Mother Nature makes me humble and prepared to face every blow courageously.

Anne's Concentration Camps

1. WESTERBORK (Holland)

Reuter, head of the SS in occupied Holland, wrote the following account to Himmler, head of the Reich police force, in 1942:

> *At last I can give you a report on the elimination of the Jews. So far we have sent twenty thousand Jews to Mauthausen and Auschwitz. There are about a hundred and twenty thousand still alive in Holland. We have established a work camp at Westerbork to which the Jews go willingly because they live and work there relatively peacefully. We haven't interfered up to now so that the greatest possible number of Jews will seek refuge there on their own accord. Many of them are still in contact with their relatives—about twenty thousand of them. I will have the relatives arrested October 1st—we know exactly where they are living. This will mean another thirty thousand people who, together with those already mentioned, will enable us to reduce by half the number of Dutch Jews by Christmas.*

2. AUSCHWITZ (Poland)

The Germans established the Auschwitz Concentration Camp where ten thousand people at a time went to the gas chambers and, according to the estimate of the camp commandant himself, no less than three million people were murdered in one way or another. Auschwitz was first built to eliminate Polish resistance fighters and then the whole unhappy population of Poland. In 1941 Himmler gave orders for it to be expanded and for the surrounding marshes to be drained. The new camp was called Birkenau and it was put to immediate use for over a hundred thousand Russian prisoners. The first Jews arrived from Silesia and Slovakia. From the very beginning the disabled were gassed in a room at the crematorium. . . In the same year, Rudolf Hess, commandant of Auschwitz, was given responsibility for "the final solution" [the elimination of all Jews].

Auschwitz was considered the most suitable camp for the physical elimination of the Jews by using gas. We have it from the notorious Hess, that more than seventy thousand Russian prisoners were put to death there. He himself states that the Germans put to death no less than ten thousand deported Jews a day. It is recorded that the death trains which arrived regularly at Auschwitz contained ninety thousand people from Slovakia, sixty-five thousand from Greece, eleven thousand from France, twenty thousand from Belgium, ninety thousand from Holland, four hundred thousand from Hungary, two hundred and fifty thousand from Poland and upper Silesia, and a hundred thousand from Germany.

ADAPTED FROM
The Scourge of the Swastika
Lord Russell of Liverpool

HISTORICAL CHRONOLOGY

Life of Anne Frank	Historical and Cultural Events
1933 The Frank family moves to Amsterdam, Holland, to escape Nazi persecution brought about by Hitler's racist laws.	**1933** January 30—Nazis win power in Germany under Hitler.
	1933-1935 Hitler establishes a Nazi dictatorship in Germany, the Third Reich. He dissolves parliament and abolishes all constitutional rights. All political parties and trade unions are abolished. The political police force, called the Gestapo, is founded, and concentration camps for the elimination of opposition are opened.

Frankfurt—Romer Square with its typical medieval atmosphere

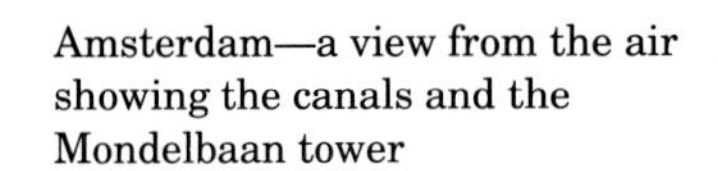

Amsterdam—a view from the air showing the canals and the Mondelbaan tower

Life of Anne Frank	Historical and Cultural Events
	1934 August—Hitler assumes full powers: he becomes head of state, Chancellor of the Reich, and head of the armed forces. He adopts the title of Führer. He establishes as state doctrine the principle of Arian racial superiority, commences the persecution of the Jews, and imposes obligatory conscription and rearmament.
1935 Ann Frank begins attending the Montessori school.	**1935-1936** Attack on, and conquest of, Ethiopia by fascist Italy.

Manuscript page from Anne Frank's diary, addressed to her imaginary friend, Kitty

Berlin—the Brandenburg Gate decorated with swastikas

Life of Anne Frank	Historical and Cultural Events
	1935- 1939 Civil war in Spain. Nazi-Fascist intervention in support of Franco. The Berlin-Rome military alliance.
	1938 Hitler annexes Austria.
1939 The Dutch government proclaims its neutrality. The Franks remain hopeful.	**1939** The Germans occupy Czechoslovakia. September 1—The Germans invade Poland. France and Britain declare war on Germany. The Second World War begins.

Guernica—painted by Pablo Picasso as a protest against Nazi involvement in Spain

The identification mark all the Jews were required to wear on their clothing

Life of Anne Frank	Historical and Cultural Events
1940 Motorized German troops and parachutists occupy strategic points in Holland. Bombing of the large cities begins. The Dutch queen and the government take refuge in London. Once again, the Franks find themselves under German rule.	**1940** April 9—Germany invades Denmark and Norway. May 10—Germany invades Holland, Belgium, and Luxembourg. June 10—Italy sides with Germany. June 22—The collapse and surrender of France. De Gaulle organizes French anti-Nazi resistance.
1941 The special Nazi laws are extended to Holland. Anne Frank is obliged to leave the Montessori school and enroll in a Jewish school. February 25-26—The people of Amsterdam strike in protest against abuse directed at the Jews.	**1941** The Germans go on to invade Rumania, Bulgaria, and Greece. June 22—Germany attacks the Soviet Union. The war escalates. December 7—The Japanese attack the American fleet at Pearl Harbor in the Hawaiian Islands. The United States is obliged to enter the war. The war spreads to Asia and Africa.

Life of Anne Frank	Historical and Cultural Events
1942 June 12—Anne is given her "diary" as a birthday gift and starts to write it in letter form. The letters are written to an imaginary friend, Kitty. July 6—Anne Frank takes refuge with her family in a secret hiding place.	**1942** December—The Russians stop the Germans at Moscow. **1942-1944** Dutch resistance fighters intensify their activity and Nazi repressive measures increase—capital punishment, mass deportation, forced labor.
	1943 January - February—The Nazis capitulate at Stalingrad. July—The Allies land in Sicily. July 25—Fascism is overthrown in Italy. September 8—Italy asks for an armistice with the United States and England and is occupied by the Germans. Mussolini establishes the Salo Republic.

The first day of the invasion of Russia—armored German troops in the Ukraine

Life of Anne Frank	Historical and Cultural Events
1944 August 4—Acting upon information provided by an informer, a Gestapo officer discovers the Frank's hiding place. They are arrested.	**1944** June 6—The Allies land in Normandy.
Early August—The Franks are sent to Westerbork, a transit camp for Jews.	**1944-1945** The Russians and the Allies make major progress in rolling back the German forces on both the Eastern and Western fronts.
September 2—Anne is moved with her family to Auschwitz (Poland) where she is separated from her father.	
October 30—Anne and Margot, now separated from their mother, are put on board a train of young prisoners headed for the concentration camp of Bergen-Belsen (Germany).	
November 9—Southern Holland is liberated by the first Allied offensive. But it is too late for Anne.	

A photograph of the Warsaw ghetto—attempts to exit were punished by death

Norway was occupied by the Germans. This photograph shows German troops at Tromso.

Life of Anne Frank	Historical and Cultural Events
1945 February—Anne and Margot succumb to typhus. March—Anne dies shortly after her sister and is buried in a communal grave at Bergen-Belsen.	**1945** April—Holland and Italy are liberated. May—Hitler commits suicide. Germany surrenders. The war ends in Europe. August 6-9—The Americans drop two atomic bombs on Japan.

Amsterdam—The building where the "Secret Annexe" was, which now houses the Anne Frank Foundation

A 1944 poster—"The blood of thousands of Poles will be avenged in battle"

Berlin—June 1945: Zukov, Montgomery, and Rokossosvkij

BOOKS FOR FURTHER READING

Anne Frank by Angela Bull, Hamish Hamilton, 1984.

Anne Frank: Life in Hiding by Johanna Hurwitz, Jewish Publication Society, 1988.

Anne Frank Remembered by Miep Giles, Simon and Schuster, 1987.

The Diary of a Young Girl by Anne Frank, Doubleday,1967.

INDEX

(Continued on page 104)

INDEX *(Continued from page 103)*